Boys Are Super Awesome!

Inspiring Short Stories for Boys About Mindfulness, Confidence, Perseverance, and Kindness

AVIA JOYCE

Thank you for buying our book!

If you find this storybook fun and useful, we would be very grateful if you could post a short review on Amazon! Your support does make a difference and we read every review personally.

If you would like to leave a review, just head on over to this book's Amazon page and click "Write a customer review."

Thank you for your support!

Table of Contents

Work Your Magic

Brady opened his eyes and saw nothing but shadows around him. His dark bedroom waited for Monday morning sunlight to peak over the horizon and shine in through the window. He sleepily turned off his alarm clock and wished he could go back to sleep as he dreaded the day ahead.

It was the start of a new week, and Brady's teacher had asked him to come to school extra early to have a serious talk. The only thing that motivated him to get to class that day was the desire to sign up for the year-end field trip to the zoo the following Monday. Today was his chance to hand in his permission form and the money he had saved for the field trip of a lifetime!

Brady wanted to go on the trip to the zoo because he absolutely loved animals. He thought about animals every single day and dreamed about them every single night. Brady loved animals so much. He had his own dog named Poppy. Poppy was a real troublemaker. When she was not making trouble, she could usually be found asleep in her dog bed beneath Brady's desk. Brady also had a horse named Journey who lived in a barn that Brady could see from his bedroom.

On that early morning, Brady dragged himself out from under his warm blanket, got ready for the day, and headed to school for the dreaded talk with his teacher. When Brady arrived at school, he walked into his classroom to see his teacher, Mr. Burvis, writing the day's lessons on the blackboard.

"Hi, Mr. Burvis. Sorry if I'm late," apologized Brady.

"No, don't worry. You're actually early," replied Mr. Burvis, "which is excellent because what I am about to tell you is top secret." The teacher quickly closed the classroom door and adjusted the blinds on the classroom windows for privacy. He turned toward Brady with a troubled look written across his face.

"Am I in trouble?" Brady asked, nervously.

"Let me cut straight to the chase, Brady. You're at risk of failing this grade and having to go to summer school," Mr. Burvis said, clearly concerned for his student. "I'm sorry to have to tell you this Brady, but summer school starts one week from today, which is the same day as the field trip to the zoo. Either you get straight As this week, or you'll have to go to summer school *and* miss the trip to the zoo."

Brady was devastated. His lower lip began to shake, and he could feel tears pool up in the corners of his eyes.

"Don't worry, Brady! I have a plan. I can keep you out of summer school," Mr. Burvis stated boldly.

"You can? Oh, Mr. Burvis, I will do anything!" Brady pleaded. "I *need*

to go on that trip! I have been looking forward to going to the zoo my whole life! I know my grades are bad but, when I do schoolwork, I panic and feel that I can't do it! School is just too hard! Please tell me your plan."

"Well, this is going to be hard to believe, so I need you to trust me," the teacher explained. "I'm a wizard and, believe it or not, I have magical powers!"

Brady looked at him in disbelief.

"I was issued a wand by the Wizardry Board, but I don't believe in using magic to solve life's problems. Since this is such a desperate situation, however, I sharpened my wand into a pencil for you to use on your assignments this week. With this magical pencil, you will have the courage, intelligence, and superb abilities to ace everything you work on."

Mr. Burvis then gave Brady the most magnificent pencil Brady had ever seen. It was a long, golden pencil with a sharp tip. Engraved on the side of the pencil were the letters HB.

"My full name is Heath Burvis," he explained while running his fingers over the letters. "I got it engraved so I can tell my wand apart from others."

Brady's jaw dropped. At first, he did not believe Mr. Burvis. But the more Mr. Burvis spoke, the more convincing he was.

"You'll have to try using the magical pencil to truly appreciate its powers. To use it, just close your eyes, blow on it like you are blowing out a birthday candle, then say, 'Come on wand, work your magic'!"

Brady took the wand into his hand. It was as light as a feather, despite its golden appearance. They decided he would try it.

As the day continued, students poured into the classroom. The bell rang, and Mr. Burvis told the students to read about animal habitats in their science textbooks. Brady was interested in habitats, so he happily read the chapter from start to finish.

"Close your books! Pop quiz time!" Mr. Burvis announced.

Brady immediately began panicking. He felt nervous and unsure of himself. He had just been told that he must improve his grades, and now there was a pop quiz.

"This is a disaster!" Brady thought to himself. "I should try the magical pencil!"

Brady held the magical pencil in his hand and hoped for the best. Once Brady received his quiz, he listened to his teacher's previous instructions and closed his eyes, took a deep breath, and blew on the magical pencil.

"Come on wand, work your magic!" Brady thought to himself. He then opened his eyes and began his pop quiz.

At the end of the day, Brady waited to receive his grade on the pop quiz. He was very worried about how he had done. As the last school bell rang, his name was finally called by his teacher. Brady walked nervously toward Mr. Burvis' desk and took the quiz into his hand. Written on the top of his quiz was a big letter A! He could not believe his eyes! He had never received an A before.

"Good work, Brady!" Mr. Burvis praised. "You got the highest mark in the whole class! Keep up the good work," he said as he winked with his twinkling green eyes.

"Class, for your homework, please hand in a drawing of someone you admire by tomorrow at eight o'clock sharp," Mr. Burvis announced.

The day was over, and Brady hurried home from school with a wide grin while regularly checking his quiz to be sure the A was still there. The work of the magical pencil had impressed Brady, and he wanted to try it again soon. He decided he would use it that evening to work on

his art project for tomorrow.

That night, Brady sat down at his desk with the magical pencil in his hand, ready to work. He closed his eyes, took a deep breath, and blew on the wand.

"Come on wand, work your magic!" he thought to himself.

Morning came, and Brady turned off his alarm clock before it went off. He had been awake for hours to put the finishing touches to his art project. The project instructions were to draw someone he admired. Of course, Brady decided to draw his dog, Poppy. Although he had used his magical pencil, he had worked very long and very hard on his sketch, and he was very proud of the outcome.

By the time Brady got to his classroom, it was packed with kids and their art. When Brady entered, the room went silent.

"What's wrong?" Brady asked.

"Your art!" one girl exclaimed.

"It's amazing!" a boy chimed in.

The classroom migrated toward Brady as they inspected and complimented his masterpiece. Brady's peers and teacher were very impressed by the sketch of Poppy, and, thanks to the magic of the wand, Brady received his second A!

By Wednesday, Brady received three additional As on assignments in math, spelling, and Spanish. Brady was so happy to be getting better grades, and he was understanding his work a lot more, but he wished he could experience this success on his own, without the magical pencil!

On Thursday evening, Brady tucked himself into bed early. He wanted to wake up before school the next day and study more for his final test, which was the last step to getting to go to the zoo with his class. He drifted off to sleep that night and dreamed of all the animals he

would see if he made it onto the year-end field trip.

It was the morning of Brady's most daunting task, the final test, and he awoke to the sound of pounding hooves. He opened his curtains and watched as his horse, Journey, ran wildly up and down the paddock. The horse was warning of a wicked storm, which was brewing above. Dark, threatening clouds rolled in and there were distant sounds of thunder.

Brady was glad he woke up early because he would have extra time to study. He got out of bed, sat at his desk, and began studying with Poppy at his feet. After hours of studying, it was time for him to stop and get ready for school. Brady felt prepared, but of course, he was still a little nervous.

"Don't worry," he thought, reassuring himself. "You have the magical pencil to get your final A!"

Brady put away his books, fed and watered his animals, and gathered his school supplies. Suddenly, there was a loud strike of lightning with a bang of thunder and—

"Where did I leave the magical pencil?!" Brady asked himself, fearfully. He looked on his desk amongst his papers, but he could not find the magical pencil he so desperately needed to pass his test.

Again, the lightning flashed, and the thunder rumbled loudly. Brady covered his ears. That's when he saw it: chewed-up, soggy pieces of the magical pencil lying upon Poppy's dog bed beneath Brady's desk.

Brady began to cry. He would not be able to go to the zoo. He would have to hear all the stories about the fun he missed both at the zoo and during the summer!

"What a disaster!" he whimpered.

When Brady got to school, he pulled Mr. Burvis aside and confessed the morning's events. He cried and apologized for ruining his wand.

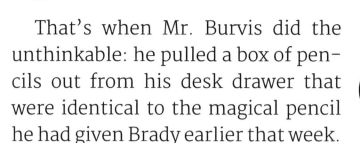

That's when Mr. Burvis did the unthinkable: he pulled a box of pencils out from his desk drawer that were identical to the magical pencil he had given Brady earlier that week.

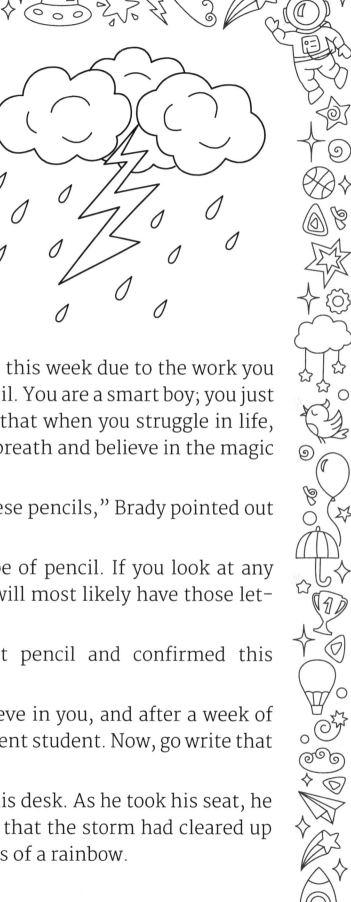

"I'm confused!" Brady said with a tear-streaked face.

"I'm sorry, Brady, but I had to fool you. I'm not a wizard, and that pencil was not magical. I told you that story because I wanted you to believe in yourself. You accomplished so much this week due to the work you put in, not due to the magic of that pencil. You are a smart boy; you just lack confidence. I wanted to show you that when you struggle in life, anything is possible if you take a deep breath and believe in the magic within yourself!"

"But your initials are engraved in these pencils," Brady pointed out sheepishly.

"HB pencils are a very common type of pencil. If you look at any pencil you have in your pencil case, it will most likely have those letters on it," Mr. Burvis replied.

Brady glanced over at the nearest pencil and confirmed this statement.

Mr. Burvis continued, "Brady, I believe in you, and after a week of straight As, I know that you're an excellent student. Now, go write that test!"

Brady turned around and walked to his desk. As he took his seat, he glanced out of the window and noticed that the storm had cleared up and the sky was smeared with the colors of a rainbow.

The class became quiet, and the test began. Brady looked over his test and felt an unfamiliar feeling: confidence. He grabbed a regular, yellow pencil from his pencil case. He closed his eyes, took a deep breath, and said to himself: "Brady, work your magic."

Believe in the magic within yourself

Max and the Picture Portal

There once was a ten-year-old boy named Max who wanted, more than anything, to leave his stressful childhood behind so he could become a happy grown-up. He thought his childhood was too hard because of his strict teachers, who assigned way too much homework, and his mean parents, who had too many rules and demands. Max felt that he spent all his time struggling to please adults, and he craved the complete freedom he knew adulthood would give him. Little did Max know that his dream to grow up would soon be possible.

Max lived in a clearing in the woods with his mom, dad, and little sister, Hanna. Max's mom was very strict and expected Max to do chores, chores, and more chores. Max felt that he could never meet his mother's expectations. Max's father also had high expectations of Max and wanted him to achieve record-breaking grades in school. His parents' impossibly high standards put the weight of the world on Max's shoulders, and he felt he would soon collapse beneath its unbearable weight.

Luckily, Max had his sister, Hanna, to rely on for emotional support. Although they were siblings, they were also best friends. They always got along well, and Hanna always knew the right thing to say to comfort Max when he felt pressured. Deep down, Max knew he would always have the love and support of his Hanna Banana, as he often called her.

One rainy day, Max walked home from school as quickly as possible because he did not want any of his classmates to find out he did not have enough money to take the bus. Max's mom had lost her job again, so his family did not have any money, which made Max feel very stressed out.

After his long walk home, Max snuggled into the covers of his bed blanket, buried his face in his pillow, and burst into tears.

"I just want to grow up!" he shouted, frustrated. He wondered when Hanna would be home so he could be hugged by the only person who understood the stress he was under.

Just then, Max heard a knock at the door. Hoping it was Hanna, unable to find her house key, he quickly went to greet her. He opened the door but found no one waiting for him. However, he did find a mysterious envelope on his doorstep that had his name on it. Max had never received his own piece of mail before, so he opened it right away. Inside the envelope was a letter.

Dear Max,

Hi. My name is Mr. Maximus. I know you go by the name 'Max' right now, but in the future, you will like to be called by your full name, 'Mr. Maximus'. I know that because I am from the future, and, I am in fact, the future YOU!

When you get older, you will host your very own television show, which will air all around the world. Your show will be a huge success and will bring you a lot of money and fame.

I am writing to you today because as the future you, I am currently overwhelmed with the TV job I just described, and I need your help!

I think you would be a better celebrity than me because you are a child with an endless supply of energy.

Can we please trade places?

11

If you are interested in being an adult, and if you want to be rich and famous, I suggest you look at the photograph I've included with this letter.

Talk to you soon.

Sincerely,

Mr. Maximus

"This must be a joke!" Max thought to himself. Just then, he saw something else poke out of the envelope. It was the photograph Mr. Maximus had mentioned. Max recognized the image right away, and he wondered how Mr. Maximus had managed to get a photograph from so many years ago.

"This can't be real," Max said aloud, questioning everything he had learned about reality.

He took a closer look at the photograph and immediately thought back to that magical summer's eve when his family played board games around their small, oak table inside their screened-in porch. That evening, they could hear the radio playing, with a backdrop of trickles coming from the nearby stream that traveled throughout the forest surrounding their house. They could smell the barbecue as it sizzled and cooked the kabobs they made as a family.

Max gently touched the image of his younger self. He looked so happy. If he remembered correctly, this photo was taken the evening he and Hanna became best friends. In that instant, the memories from the photograph washed away his worries, and made him feel at peace.

"Will life ever be like that again?" he wondered, as he soaked up the happiness of the photograph. As Max absorbed every pixel of the

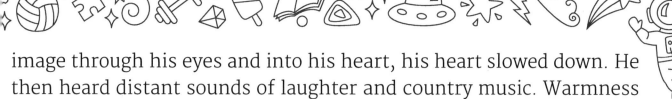

image through his eyes and into his heart, his heart slowed down. He then heard distant sounds of laughter and country music. Warmness rapidly took over his body, and then, he fell asleep.

Max awoke and slowly opened his eyes, piecing his surroundings together like a jigsaw puzzle. He heard giggles blended with the sound of country music, and he smelled fresh kabobs. He was in a forest, and, to his right, a strange man sat staring happily at Max with a big mustache perfectly framing his wide smile.

"Hi, Max! I'm so glad you decided to come!" said the stranger, excitedly.

"Who are you?" Max asked, confused.

"I'm Mr. Maximus, the man who wrote you the letter! I'm the future you!"

"You can't be from the future. I don't believe you!" Max replied.

"I'll prove it!" said Mr. Maximus. He took Max's arm and walked him along a stream to a very familiar place—home. Inside Max's screened-in porch were four younger versions of the members of his little family. They were playing games around their oak table while eating kabobs.

"If you're the future me, and I'm the present me, then who is that?" Max pointed to the young boy who giggled and played games with Max's family within the screened-in porch.

"That's you from the past," Mr. Maximus explained. "We are actually inside the photograph I included in the letter I sent to you."

Max looked at Mr. Maximus, confused.

"Allow me to explain," Mr. Maximus went on. "You see, everyone has special moments in life that determine the type of person that they will become. When we capture these moments in photographs, they become picture portals. A picture portal is a meeting spot where

past, present, and future versions of one person can gather and discuss life's important issues."

Max looked at his little family from the past. Everything was just as he remembered. He began to believe what Mr. Maximus claimed.

"Why did you bring me here?" asked Max.

"Like I explained in the letter, I need you to go to the future and take my place as an adult, while I go to the past and be a kid. I'm in way over my head in the future with the television show I'm hosting. You would be a lot better at it than me because you have a lot more energy than I do. Also, I know you want to be a grown-up, and now you can!"

"When you get to the future and I get to the past, the magic of this picture portal will change our appearances. Therefore, I'll look identical to you, and you'll look identical to me. It's the perfect plan," Mr. Maximus explained.

Max wanted to be happy like he was in the past, but his current homework and chore demands were so overwhelming that he felt it would be impossible to ever feel that way again.

"Anything is better than being a kid!" he thought to himself.

At that moment, Max decided to do the bravest thing he had ever done. He firmly grasped Mr. Maximus' outstretched hand, shook it, and said: "It's a deal, Mr. Maximus." As Max and Mr. Maximus shook hands, they disappeared.

"What a weird dream that was!" Max said as he woke up the following morning. He sat up, opened his eyes, and realized he was in a strange room.

"Where am I?" Max panicked. He put his hand to his chin to think deeply about what had happened, and he noticed his face felt unusually rough. Alarmed, he ran to a nearby mirror and looked at himself in horror as reality hit him.

"I've turned into Mr. Maximus!" Max exclaimed. Indeed, Max looked exactly as Mr. Maximus had appeared in the picture portal. Max was officially a grown-up.

"I have a mustache," he thought as he felt the scruffy hair on his face. He ran his fingers through the thinning hair on his head, and over the wrinkles surrounding his tired eyes. He then stepped away from the mirror and looked at his new body. He was tall now, but he had some of the same features as before, such as the same thin frame, knobbly knees, and unusually long legs. His striped pajamas hung loosely off his body and 'Mr. Maximus' was professionally embroidered on the shirt pocket.

Max peeled his eyes away from his new body and focused on the strange room he was in. It was a huge bedroom with a big bed full of pillows. To his left, the entire wall was a giant television. Another wall was completely covered with cabinets, which were packed with video-gaming equipment. The gaming systems in the cabinets were so advanced, Max had never heard of any of them before.

After looking around his dream bedroom, Max moved on to see the rest of Mr. Maximus' house. He carefully opened the bedroom door and was shocked to see the house was actually a mansion that had been transformed into a gigantic, indoor waterpark! The waterpark resembled a jungle-like courtyard in the middle of the mansion. The courtyard was overlooked by surrounding rooms with balconies, which acted as openings for water slides and diving boards to jut out into the water below. A lazy river also flowed throughout, which took swimmers to a carnival in the backyard.

In the backyard, Max saw merry-go-rounds, roller coasters, and animals like lions, chimpanzees, and even elephants! While exploring, Max also stumbled upon the front gates of Mr. Maximus' property. Screaming fans reached for Max through the gates, with signs declaring their love for Mr. Maximus. Max could clearly see that the future him had a lot of fans.

"This is a dream come true! Being an adult is just as I imagined!" Max exclaimed. He spent all day exploring Mr. Maximus' mansion, and he was so distracted, he did not miss his old life at all.

Around eight o'clock that evening, Max heard a noise coming from the kitchen. The sound was Mr. Maximus' telephone ringing.

"Hello?" Max answered.

"Hi, Honey," replied the caller. Max recognized that voice: it was his mom.

"Hi, Mom! It's getting late. When are you coming home?" asked Max.

"Home?" she replied. "I am home, honey. I moved away last year. Did you forget?" She asked, concerned.

"Oh, of course not!" responded Max, trying to hide his shock. "Can you remind me why you moved?"

"Your father and I moved because we could not handle the fame, honey. You're so famous now that everywhere we went, the paparazzi and fans would swarm us and take pictures of us. So, we got disguises, changed our names, and moved to another country. You still have Hanna living nearby. She's away on a business trip right now though."

"Are you feeling okay, honey?" she asked.

"Yes, I'm fine," Max lied. A single tear rolled down Max's cheek. "I have to go. I love you," he said, too heartbroken to carry on the conversation.

Nine o'clock in the evening came. Throughout the day, Max had played many futuristic video games and swam a lot in the waterpark, so he was tired. Before bed, he decided to make a giant sandwich. After all, he would have to learn to make delicious meals if he was going to act like he was Mr. Maximus, the world's greatest TV chef.

After eating, Max crawled into bed and waited to fall asleep. In that moment, he felt very alone. He had never spent a night away from his mom or dad or Hanna before, and he realized he may never see his mom or dad again. He missed his family, so he called his mom, using Mr. Maximus' phone, but she did not answer Max's calls. Max called his mom over and over that night just to hear the recording of his mom's voice as she said: "Please leave a message after the beep."

The next morning, Max woke up in a pool of his own tears, which reminded him he was now living the adult life of Mr. Maximus. He walked sleepily to the kitchen and quickly noticed the complete mess he had left for himself from the night before. There were dishes in the sink, crumbs on the counter, and ingredients he had left out. He realized that, without his mother's chore chart and constant cleaning reminders, it was hard to keep a clean house.

"I'll clean later," he thought to himself, enjoying the fact that his mom could not make him clean right this minute. He then made a bowl of cereal and sat down for breakfast.

As Max slurped the last drops of milk from his cereal bowl, Mr. Maximus' phone rang. It was a man who introduced himself as Mr. Maximus' boss. He told Max that the following day, he was expected to host his live television show to share his famous Ooey Gooey Pie recipe with the world. He had to memorize the recipe, then bake the pie on television while he shared cooking tips and techniques with the audience. The man also told Max that Mr. Maximus' fans had waited a long time to see the secret way to make this pie, so if the episode was not successful, Mr. Maximus would be fired, and his fame and fortune would disappear.

Max was stunned by the strict man, and he panicked as he had never made a pie before. He had no idea where to start.

The phone rang again, and Max answered nervously, as he was afraid it was the man again. This time, however, it was his sister, Hanna. He was relieved to hear her voice. She told him she was home from her business trip, and she was on her way over to his house to catch up. Max looked forward to Hanna's visit because, on top of being very stressed, he was very homesick.

Hanna arrived, and Max was shocked to see his little sister as an adult. She wore a blue business suit and looked very professional. Upon greeting her at the door, Hanna took many photos of herself and Max. She posed and smiled in a fake manner as she took picture after picture with her brother. At first, Max thought it was just his little sister innocently trying to make lasting memories, but he soon realized that she was taking photos to sell on the internet. Hanna had changed. She was not the same Hanna he knew from childhood. She was distant and did not have her older brother's interests at heart. She was no longer Max's friend; she was just another one of Mr. Maximus' fans.

It was the morning of the day Max was going to bake the Ooey Gooey Pie for the whole world on live TV. He was terrified because he had finally become a wealthy adult, and he could already lose his job, just like his mom had in his past life. As soon as Max woke up, he sat down at Mr. Maximus' computer and searched for the Ooey Gooey Pie recipe. After hours of browsing the computer, Max found the recipe in a file entitled 'Secret Recipes'. He read the recipe over and over, and tried his best to memorize it, as Mr. Maximus' boss had told him to.

Since Max had never cooked anything before, he watched educational videos and practiced baking basics all day to get more familiar with the use of kitchen appliances. Max was glad that in his past life, his teachers and dad had taught him to study effectively. The skill of being able to learn new information really prepared him for this

moment.

After practicing, he realized the kitchen was messier than any kitchen he had ever seen before. He decided to make himself a chore chart, just like the one his mother used in his past. The chart would help him keep the kitchen, and the rest of the mansion, in top shape from then on.

That evening, Max arrived at the TV studio feeling overwhelmed and exhausted from his attempt to memorize and perfect every detail of the Ooey Gooey Pie recipe in one day. Before he knew it, he was dressed and in front of a live audience with blaring lights and cameras staring at him from every angle.

"Action!" the director yelled. The show began, and Max actually did well with reading his lines on the teleprompter. His Ooey Gooey Pie was turning out beautifully.

"The secret to the Ooey Gooey Pie is the very last step," Max explained to the audience. "Here you roast the outer marshmallows with an old-fashioned blow-torch!" Max said, nervously holding the blowtorch as his hands shook. The audience leaned in, interested to see him demonstrate the use of such an outdated device. Max lit the blowtorch and began waving it back and forth above the outer marshmallow layer of the pie when, suddenly, he dropped the torch! The torch rolled to the side and touched the kitchen

floor mat, setting it on fire!

The fire spread quickly throughout the studio set, and the whole place had to be evacuated. No one got hurt, but Max was so embarrassed that he secretly hopped back in the limo and went back to the mansion.

At the mansion, Max found a letter waiting for him on the front doorstep. Although everyone in his future life had called him Mr. Maximus, this letter had Max written on it in bold, red letters. Max opened the letter and began to read.

Dear Max,

Please meet me in the picture portal. It's urgent.

Sincerely,

Mr. Maximus

Max looked at the photograph that came with the letter. He realized it was the exact same photograph as the one he was sent last time. He looked hard at his family in the picture. Again, they were happily playing board games together on the porch. He saw the happiness on the face of the boy he once was.

"Maybe childhood isn't that bad," he thought to himself. "After all, I'm even more miserable as an adult than I was as a child! On top of being unhappy and stressed, I now have no one to talk to. I have no mom, no dad, and no Hanna! I want to be a kid again!" Max admitted.

Max stared into the photograph and heard country music. Before he knew it, he was back in the picture portal discussing life with Mr. Maximus.

Like Max, Mr. Maximus had struggled to live life as a child. He did not like being told what to do, and he thought he had too much homework. Therefore, Max and Mr. Maximus decided they would switch back to their original lives. They shook on their new deal and disappeared from the picture portal.

When Mr. Maximus returned to adulthood, he got his show back on the air by winning over his boss' tastebuds with fresh, sizzling kabobs. In the present, Max's mom had a list of chores for him to do right away, and his teacher assigned him heaps of homework. Max hugged each of his family members extra tight that night. By using the picture portal, Max and Mr. Maximus had learned to appreciate the life they were living, exactly as it was. Mr. Maximus was glad to finally be an adult again, and, in this moment, Max was perfectly happy to be a kid.

Enjoy being a kid

Nice Thinking, Andy!

Andy was a very busy kid. There were lots and lots of things that he had to do every day.

He had to feed his bird, Paco.

He had to pack his backpack and go to school.

He had to help his little sister, Allison, get on and off of the bus.

He had to clear the dishes from the table after supper.

Not only did Andy have lots of things that kept him busy every day, but there were lots of decisions that Andy had to make every day too.

In fact, the older that Andy got, the more choices he had to make for himself.

Andy liked the feeling of being in charge of some things, and he always tried to make the best choice. Sometimes, there were lots of different things that Andy had to think about before he made a final decision.

Like last week when Andy had been cleaning up his room. First, he had put away all of his socks. Then, he stacked his books neatly on his bedside table. As he was cleaning his shelves, he came across his old stuffed rabbit.

Andy looked at the rabbit, trying to think of the last time he had played with it. It had been a long time. Allison was always asking to play with the old stuffed toy. Andy thought that he might have a decision to make about the rabbit. Before he did, he wanted to be sure and think it through carefully.

The rabbit used to be Andy's favorite toy. It would be hard to give up

such a special friend. That would be a bad thing about giving it away.

The rabbit did take up a lot of room on Andy's shelf. He was running out of space for his collection of rocket ships. That would be a good thing about giving it away.

Allison loved the rabbit so much. She always took such good care of it whenever Andy let her play with it. The rabbit would make her so happy. That would be a good thing about giving it away.

Andy weighed up the decision carefully. There was one bad thing about giving the rabbit away, and two good things about giving the rabbit away.

He decided he would give the rabbit to Allison.

Nice thinking, Andy!

Another instance was two nights ago, when Andy was finishing his supper. He had eaten all of his chicken and his mashed potatoes. All that was left was a big pile of peas. Andy thought that he might have a decision to make about the peas. Before he did, he wanted to be sure and think it through carefully.

Andy didn't really like the taste of peas. He usually had to choke them down with a glass of water. It seemed like it took him forever to finish them. That would be a bad thing about finishing his peas.

He knew that the peas were good for him. They would give his body the vitamins that it needed, and they would help him to grow strong. That would

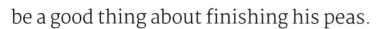

be a good thing about finishing his peas.

His mother had said that he could have chocolate pudding for dessert if he finished everything on his plate, including his peas. If he finished his peas, he would get to have dessert. That would be another good thing about finishing his peas.

Andy weighed up the decision carefully. There were two good things about finishing his peas, and one bad thing about finishing his peas.

Andy decided to finish his peas.

Nice thinking, Andy!

Another time was last Thursday, when it had been raining outside. Andy opened his closet door to grab his tennis shoes before school. When he did, he saw his yellow rain boots standing at the back of the closet. Andy thought that he might have a decision to make about the rain boots. Before he did, he wanted to make sure and think it through carefully.

Andy knew that the rain boots would keep his feet warm and dry in the damp weather. If he wore his tennis shoes, his feet would be soggy and wet before he even made it to the bus stop. That would be a good thing about wearing his rain boots to school.

Andy didn't have very many opportunities to wear his rain boots. Most days he just wore his tennis shoes. It would be kind of fun to wear something different. That would be a good thing about wearing his rain boots to school.

Unfortunately, the rain boots weren't as comfortable as Andy's tennis shoes. They pinched his toes a little, and they weren't as easy to run in. That would be a bad thing about wearing his rain boots to school.

Andy weighed up the decision carefully. There was one bad thing about wearing his rain boots to school, and two good things about wearing his rain boots to school.

Andy decided to wear his rain boots.

Nice thinking, Andy!

Andy certainly had a lot of choices to make in any day's time, and sometimes it could be tough to make a final decision.

Though every once in a while, Andy would be faced with a choice that wasn't hard to make at all.

Like last night when his family had gone out for ice cream.

The woman working behind the counter had asked Andy if he would like to have chocolate ice cream or strawberry ice cream.

Andy thought about it for just a few seconds before quickly replying, "Both!"

Nice thinking, Andy!

Be kind
to your brother
or sister

Daniel Figures It Out!

Daniel enjoyed spending time with his grandfather. His grandfather was kind, funny, and very, very, smart. Whenever Daniel had a problem, or had to make an important decision, his grandfather always knew just what to say.

Not only was he smart, but Daniel loved the actual words his grandfather would use when giving advice. Like the time when he was frustrated with teaching his dog, Sarge, how to do tricks.

Daniel had read a book called *How to Train Dogs.* He had bought all sorts of dog treats for Sarge, and he had worked with him every afternoon for six weeks. Still, Sarge wouldn't learn even the simplest command, like "sit".

When Daniel was relaying his frustrations to his grandfather one afternoon, his grandfather had simply said, "Well Daniel, you can lead a horse to water, but you can't make him drink."

At first, Daniel didn't understand. They were talking about dogs, not horses. But after he really thought about it, Daniel realized that what his grandfather meant was that he could provide every opportunity to help Sarge to learn, but he really couldn't make the dog do anything that the dog didn't want to do.

Even though Sarge still didn't know how to sit, his grandfather's words somehow helped Daniel to feel better.

His grandfather often gave guidance in some pretty interesting ways, and, if he thought about it long enough, Daniel could usually figure it out.

There was just one thing that his grandfather sometimes said that Daniel didn't quite understand. He would always say, "You can't control everything, but you can control how you respond to everything."

That didn't make any sense to Daniel. Control everything? Control your response?

Daniel was confused. Still, Daniel valued his grandfather's wisdom and valued his advice.

One Monday morning, after spending the weekend with his grandfather, Daniel woke up to a rainstorm pouring down outside of his window.

"Oh no!" thought Daniel to himself. "This rain is going to ruin everything!"

Daniel had lots of plans for the day, starting with walking to school. He knew that he'd get soaked. The rainstorm also meant that the class would have to have indoor recess, which everyone disliked. Worst of all, if it kept up, they'd have to cancel the championship soccer game that evening. His team had worked so hard to make it to the big game.

Daniel was so angry at the rain. He felt like screaming. He felt like crying. He felt like tearing the pages out of his science book. He felt like throwing his granola bar across the room.

Just as Daniel was feeling all of these uncomfortable feelings, and thinking about doing these destructive things, he heard his grandfather's advice in his head.

"You can't control everything, but you can control how you respond to everything."

Daniel thought for a moment. Could he control the rain? No, he couldn't. No one could.

But he could control how he responded to the rain.

29

He was in control of his body. He was in control of whether or not he ripped the pages out of his science book. He was in control of whether or not he threw his granola bar across the room.

Daniel took a deep breath and calmed himself down. He decided not to rip the pages out of the book or throw the granola bar.

Still feeling a little upset, Daniel grabbed his umbrella and set off for his soggy walk to school. By the time he got there, the rain had almost stopped, and he was feeling much better.

That afternoon at lunch, the cafeteria was serving liver and onions. Ugh! Daniel hated liver and onions! In fact, Daniel didn't know a single person who liked liver and onions. Why would they serve this? Now he would have to go hungry!

The more he thought about it, the angrier he got. He felt like causing a fuss to the cafeteria workers. He felt like sneaking two extra glasses of milk to make up for the distasteful meal. He felt like dumping his tray full of food right out on the counter.

Once again, as Daniel was thinking all of these unpleasant thoughts, he heard his grandfather's words.

"You can't control everything, but you can control how you respond to everything."

Daniel thought for a moment. Could he control what the cafeteria was serving for lunch? No, he couldn't. That wasn't his job. But he could control how he responded to what they were serving.

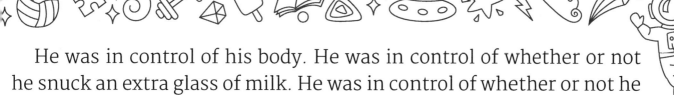

He was in control of his body. He was in control of whether or not he snuck an extra glass of milk. He was in control of whether or not he dumped his tray in the middle of the table.

Daniel took a deep breath and calmed himself down. He decided not to take the extra glass of milk or dump his tray. Instead, he grabbed a peanut butter and jelly sandwich and an apple from the cold lunch selections.

As he munched on his sandwich, Daniel thought that he may be starting to understand what his grandfather had meant about not controlling everything and only controlling his response.

By the time that school had let out, the rain had completely stopped and the soccer field had dried out enough for his team to play in the championship game.

Daniel and his teammates were very excited. They knew that they would easily beat the other team. But the other team was much better than they had anticipated. After lots of hard work by both teams, Daniel's team lost the game by just one point.

For the third time that day, Daniel was so upset that he could scream. He felt like kicking the ball far over the gates and into the tall grass that surrounded the field. He felt like snatching the championship trophy from the other team.

Before he could think any more negative thoughts, he heard his grandfather's voice.

"You can't control everything,

but you can control how you respond to everything."

Daniel thought for a moment. Could he control the fact that his team had lost the game? No, he couldn't. It was too late for that. But he could control how he responded to the loss.

He was in control of his body. He was in control of whether or not he kicked the ball over the gates. He was in control of whether or not he snatched the trophy from the other team.

Daniel took a deep breath and calmed himself down. He decided not to kick the ball or snatch the trophy. Instead, he graciously congratulated the other team on their big win.

As Daniel turned to walk off the field, his grandfather was waiting for him next to the bleachers. Daniel brightened a bit at the sight of him.

"Great game, Daniel! I'm so proud of you. You really gave it a good effort," congratulated his grandfather.

"Yeah, I guess," replied Daniel. "But we still lost, and I still feel pretty awful about it."

"There's always next year, Daniel. The important thing is that you had fun and, maybe, learned a little something along the way. Did you learn anything?" asked his grandfather.

"Actually, I did, Grandpa. I learned it from you," said Daniel.

"From me? I was just sitting in the stands. What could I have taught you?" his grandfather questioned.

"I think I finally understand what you mean when you say that I can't control everything, but I can control how I respond to everything," Daniel explained.

"Oh that!" said his grandfather knowingly. "Not only am I proud of how you played, but I'm proud of how you acted when you didn't win."

"That's what you taught me, Grandpa. And not just the game, but

everything—the rain, my lunch. I'm learning there are lots of things that I can't control," said Daniel.

"But you can control how you respond," added his grandfather.

"That's right, Grandpa! And right now, I'm going to respond by giving you the biggest bear hug I can!"

Under the lights of the field, Daniel wrapped his arms around his grandfather and gave him a huge hug.

Aunt Marti and the Glitter Globe

Sometimes Trey felt a little nervous.

If he knew that he had a big test at school, sometimes his stomach would hurt.

If he knew that he would have to sing in the choir concert, sometimes his heart would beat fast.

If he thought his dad would be late picking him up, sometimes he would breathe a little faster and a little heavier.

Trey didn't like how he felt when he was nervous. In fact, sometimes he even felt nervous about getting nervous.

When he felt like this, Trey knew that there were lots of people he could talk to who would help him to feel better. His parents were great listeners, and they always knew just what to say. His fifth-grade teacher, Ms. Bonner, could always help Trey too. Even Trey's Grandma and Grandpa always seemed to know just what to do to help him to calm down.

Trey's very favorite person to talk to when he was feeling nervous was his Aunt Marti. She was kind, gentle, and smart. Sometimes Trey thought that she might understand him even better than his own parents.

One of the best things about his Aunt Marti was that her apartment was just a few blocks away from his house. If he didn't have basketball practice after school, he would often stop in for a quick visit.

His Aunt Marti had a big fluffy cat named Sampson who always jumped right up into Trey's lap. Aunt Marti would always make him a fancy cup of tea, just like she did for grown-ups. And she'd always stir it with a piece of black licorice. They'd sit at her small kitchen table together and she'd ask Trey all about his day. She was always so interested in everything he had to say, and she always gave him the best advice and ideas. His Aunt Marti always made him feel so very special.

One afternoon, after a particularly rough day, Trey thought it best that he stop in and see Aunt Marti on his way home.

He walked up the three flights of steps to her apartment and knocked on the door. His aunt looked through the tiny peephole. When she saw that it was Trey, she flung open the door and wrapped her arms around him.

"My favorite nephew!" she exclaimed. "Come in, come in!"

"Hi, Aunt Marti," said Trey quietly.

"What's wrong, my love?" asked his aunt with concern. "I can tell that you aren't yourself."

"It was just a tough day, that's all," replied Trey.

"Sit down and let me make you some tea. I want to hear all about it," Aunt Marti said gently.

Just being in his Aunt's apartment made Trey feel better. As soon as he sat down at the table, Sampson jumped up into his lap. That made him feel better, too.

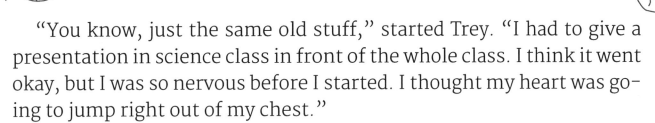

"You know, just the same old stuff," started Trey. "I had to give a presentation in science class in front of the whole class. I think it went okay, but I was so nervous before I started. I thought my heart was going to jump right out of my chest."

"Oh yes, I remember once in college that I passed out before I had to give a speech in my public speaking class," said Aunt Marti. "Did anything else happen today?"

"I got really anxious in gym class. We were playing kickball and the team captains lined up all the kids and picked teams, one by one. I was so afraid that no one would pick me. My stomach was doing backflips," reported Trey.

"That's the worst! I'm sorry that you had to deal with that," said his aunt.

"It's alright. I'm just glad that the day is over, and I can finally relax," said Trey, taking a sip of his tea.

"Hey, Trey, I've been meaning to show you something. Hold on just a second," said his aunt as she disappeared into her bedroom at the back of the apartment.

She returned just a few seconds later holding something small and shiny in her hands.

"What do you have there, Aunt Marti?" Trey asked, his interest peaked.

Aunt Marti held the item out to Trey. It was round, like a ball, and made out of glass. It was filled with water on the inside. Floating around in the water were thousands of tiny flakes of silver glitter. It fit perfectly in Aunt Marti's open palm.

"Wow!" exclaimed Trey. "That's so cool! What is it?"

"This is my glitter globe," replied Aunt Marti.

"What do you do with it?" asked Trey.

"Well, when I'm feeling nervous or anxious, it helps me to calm down," Aunt Marti said.

"How does it do that?" asked Trey, feeling a little confused.

"Let me show you," said Aunt Marti as she gently shook the globe up and down.

When she did, the glitter loosened from where it had been resting at the bottom of the ball. It danced and shimmered, completely filling the globe.

"Think of it this way," began Aunt Marti. "When we feel upset or nervous, sometimes our insides feel all shaken up. Things feel unsettled, right? Just like the inside of this globe when I shake it."

"I understand. That's exactly what my stomach feels like when I'm nervous," said Trey, pointing to the glitter floating wildly around the globe.

"Now, take a moment to really focus on the glitter as it settles toward the bottom of the globe. As you watch, take a deep breath in through your nose and then blow it out through your mouth," instructed Aunt Marti. "With a little time, the glitter starts to calm down. You might feel like you are starting to calm down, too."

Aunt Marti handed the glass ball to Trey, "Now you try it."

Trey took the globe from his aunt and gave it a few gentle shakes. He watched the glitter as it jumped up from the bottom of the globe and swirled around and around inside the ball. Once again, the wild flashes of glitter reminded Trey of how his insides felt when he was nervous.

"Focus on the glitter as it settles. Watch it swirl all the way down to the bottom," said Aunt Marti in a soothing voice. "Breathe in and out. Feel yourself calm down, just like the glitter."

Trey continued to watch the globe, taking deep breaths, in and out. By the time the last flakes of glitter had finally reached the bottom of the ball, Trey felt perfectly still and calm. The globe was perfectly still and calm too.

"That's amazing, Aunt Marti!" said Trey. "That really helped to calm me down."

"I'm glad it helped, Trey," replied Aunt Marti. "It always works for me."

Trey glanced at the clock on the microwave.

"I guess I better head out, Aunt Marti. Mom will wonder where I'm at. Thanks for letting me hang out," Trey said sincerely.

"No problem, my love. I'm glad that you stopped over," Aunt Marti said. "Oh Trey, one more thing. Why don't you take that globe with you?"

"I couldn't," answered Trey.

"Of course, you can," said Aunt Marti. "Just promise me that you'll use it whenever you're feeling nervous. And maybe someday when you have a nephew, you can give it to him."

"Definitely!" said Trey, holding the glass ball carefully as he hugged his aunt goodbye.

Trey made his way back down the three flights of stairs to the street below and started the short walk home. He watched the sun sinking behind the clouds as he wrapped his fingers gently around the globe. He noticed how calm everything around him felt. Though he couldn't be certain, he was almost sure that he saw a few flakes of glitter settling with the sunset.

Keep calm
and carry on

Fooled Ya! Fooled Ya!

Most of the time, Joshua was a pretty good kid. He usually listened to whatever his parents had to say. He usually got his chores done every day after school. He usually paid attention when his fifth-grade teacher, Mr. Jacobson, explained the homework assignment, and he usually turned that homework in on time. Yes, Joshua was usually a pretty good kid.

He had just one problem. Joshua liked to play jokes on people. Jokes aren't always a bad thing. In fact, jokes can be really funny! But Joshua liked to trick people with his jokes. He would often make up stories or say things that weren't true. Sometimes, Joshua's stories were a little scary. Once Joshua had convinced people that his stories were true, he would watch as they became nervous and then yell, "Fooled ya! Fooled ya!"

No one thought that Joshua's jokes were funny. No one except for Joshua, that is.

One Monday morning Joshua awoke early for school. As he was brushing his teeth, he came up with a plan to fool as many people as possible that day.

He started at the breakfast table with his father.

Joshua took a bite of his apple, and then yelled.

"Yee-ouch, Dad! My tooth! My tooth! I lost my tooth when I bit into this apple! Help me find it!"

Alarmed, Joshua's father dropped the newspaper he was reading and immediately began searching for Joshua's missing tooth.

"Oh no! Joshua! Are you okay? Is it bleeding? Does it hurt?" he asked with great concern in his voice.

"Fooled ya! Fooled ya!" screeched Joshua with a laugh.

"Oh Joshua, not another one of your tricks," sighed his father, feeling a mix of relief and annoyance.

"I was just teasing, Dad," joked Joshua.

"Your tricks are going to get you in trouble one of these days. Now off to the bus!" his father said sternly.

Joshua was still giggling to himself as he grabbed his backpack and headed out to catch the bus.

As Joshua stepped onto the bus, he smiled as he thought of his next trick.

He took a seat toward the back. They hadn't gone too far when Joshua began yelling at the bus driver, Ms. Tonya.

"Ms. Tonya! Ms. Tonya! There's a mouse on the bus! There's a mouse on the bus! I saw it run under Bridget's seat!" exclaimed Joshua.

Bridget screamed and jumped up on top of her seat.

Brian dropped to his hands and knees, hoping to catch a glimpse of the mouse.

Malcolm began stomping his feet in an attempt to scare the mouse.

All of the other kids erupted in squeals, while Ms. Tonya slammed on the brakes.

"Alright, everyone, just stay calm!" Ms. Tonya instructed loudly.

The children did not stay calm.

Joshua watched the chaos for a moment before yelling, "Fooled ya! Fooled ya!"

"Oh Joshua, not again," sighed Ms. Tonya. "All of your tricks are going to get you in trouble someday."

Joshua just smiled, thinking how clever he was to be able to fool everyone.

He continued his game all day long.

He fooled the gym teacher, Coach Holmes, into thinking that he had sprained his ankle.

He fooled the lunch lady, Ms. Gertrude, into thinking that his classmate Tori had taken three slices of pizza.

He fooled the custodian, Mr. Markley, into thinking that the water fountain was leaking.

Every time that his friends and teachers would become concerned, he'd yell, "Fooled ya! Fooled ya!"

And they would always remind him that all of his tricks might just get him into trouble someday.

Joshua didn't think that would ever happen.

Joshua lay in bed that night, going over all of the funny tricks he had played that day. He was feeling very proud of himself when, all of the sudden, he heard a sound just outside his bedroom window.

Tap, tap, tap.

Tap, tap, tap.

At first, Joshua couldn't believe what he was hearing. Surely there wouldn't be anyone tapping on his bedroom window. It was pitch black outside.

He lay perfectly still, hoping not to hear the sound again.

Tap, tap, tap.

Tap, tap, tap.

This time, it sounded a little bit louder, and a little closer.

Joshua pulled his covers up over his head. He was feeling really scared now. He waited.

Tap, tap, tap.

Tap, tap, tap.

Joshua couldn't stand it any longer!

"Mom! Dad!" he yelled. "There's someone outside of my window! They keep tapping on the glass! They're trying to sneak into the house! Help!"

Joshua's mother and father were watching the news in the living room. They exchanged annoyed glances and rolled their eyes. They were sure that this was just another of Joshua's tricks.

His mother didn't move from her spot on the couch as she yelled toward Joshua's bedroom.

"Joshua, I'm not falling for any more of your tricks. Now go to sleep."

"I'm serious!" Joshua yelled back.

"Sure you are, Joshua," his father replied sarcastically. "Now, I don't want to hear another word."

Joshua lay in his bed trembling. The sound came again.

Tap, tap, tap.

Tap, tap, tap.

Joshua was feeling very regretful. Everybody had been right. His tricks had gotten him into trouble!

Tap, tap, tap.

Tap, tap, tap.

He couldn't stand it any longer! He shot up from his bed and darted out into the living room.

"I'm so, so sorry!" began Joshua with tears rolling down his cheeks. "You were right! I shouldn't have played all of those tricks! I promise, I'll never, ever, play another trick again. But you have to believe me! There is someone tapping on my window!"

Joshua's parents could see the fear in his eyes and hear the desperation in his voice. They had never seen him like this before. He must be telling the truth.

His mother put her arm around his shoulder.

"It's okay Joshua. We believe you. We'll get this figured out," she said soothingly.

"I'll go check it out, okay buddy?" promised Joshua's father.

His father grabbed a flashlight and slipped out of the back door while Joshua waited on the couch, snuggled up next to his mother.

A few minutes later, his father returned, chuckling as he closed the door behind him.

"Well, Joshua, I think you are the one who got tricked this time," his father said as he held up a long, skinny branch. "It was nothing more than the wind blowing this branch against your window."

"That's all it was?" asked Joshua incredulously.

"That's it," said his dad.

"I'm glad it wasn't anything serious," said his mom. "But I do want you to remember how it felt to be a little scared and a little nervous. It didn't feel very good, did it?" asked his mother.

"No, not at all," answered Joshua.

"And, we had a hard time believing you because you'd told us so many stories in the past," added his father.

"I understand now," said Joshua. "I don't think I'll be playing tricks anymore."

"That better not be another one of your stories," his father said, gently.

"I promise. It's not," said Joshua with a wink. "No fooling."

What goes around, comes around

Albert's Notebook

"Albert! You're going to miss the school bus!" called Albert's mother from the bottom of the stairs.

"Oh no!" thought Albert as he searched under his bed for his missing left sock. "I'm gonna be late again!"

Albert gave up on the sock and rushed to the bathroom to brush his teeth and comb his hair. Of course, he was out of toothpaste and his comb was missing.

"Let's go, Albert!" he heard his mother call again.

"I'm coming!" Albert yelled back, as he tumbled out of the bathroom and down the stairs.

"Meet me in the kitchen. I've got a bagel for you," she called over her shoulder as she hurried off to the kitchen.

When Albert finally made it to the kitchen, his mother was not surprised to see that he was nowhere near ready for school.

"Oh Albert, not again," she said. "This is the third time this week that you're going to be late."

"I'm not late, Mom. I'm right on time," reasoned Albert, taking a bite of the cinnamon bagel his mother had prepared for him.

"Hardly, Albert," she replied. "Your hair isn't combed. You've only got one sock on. And I would guess that you haven't brushed your teeth yet, either. You're going to be late."

His mother was right.

"Sorry, Mom. I'm not sure what happened. I'm not doing it on

purpose," Albert said with regret in his voice.

"I know you're not, Honey. We've got to work on this," his mother said as she gently brushed his uncombed hair out of his eyes. "But not right now. We don't have time. We'll talk about it more this evening."

"Alright, Mom," Albert said, still feeling bad. "And I really am sorry."

"Don't let it ruin your day, Albert. I know that being 11 can be pretty tough sometimes. We'll figure this out together," she said, giving his hair one last tousle. "Now scoot!"

Much of Albert's day went the same way his morning had gone.

He left his lunch on the bus.

He didn't have any sharpened pencils for his math test.

He left his dirty gym clothes in his locker.

He finished the wrong assignment in his science book.

And he missed the bus to take him home.

Albert shuffled down the sidewalk, feeling sorry for himself and slowly making his way toward home.

When he finally got there, 30 minutes later than usual, his mother was waiting for him at the kitchen table with two chocolate chip cookies and a glass of milk.

Albert wasn't even hungry.

"You're a little late, aren't you?" she asked softly.

"Yes," replied Albert quietly.

"I bet I know what happened. You missed the bus again, didn't you?" his mother continued.

"I did," said Albert, feeling very defeated. "I don't like being this way, always running late and forgetting things. It doesn't feel very good."

"I know it doesn't, Albert. I promised you we'd figure this out, and we will," she said hopefully.

"How?" asked Albert desperately.

"I have something for you," she said, pulling a small black notebook out of the kitchen drawer.

"What's that? Something else for me to lose?" asked Albert skeptically.

"No, it's just the opposite. It's to help you keep track of things," his mother said excitedly.

"How does that work?" Albert questioned.

"One of the best ways to stay organized is to make a list," explained his mother. "Here, let me show you."

Albert's mother flipped open the small book. She had created several lists and charts within the notebook:

Night Before School:

	Sunday	Monday	Tuesday	Wednesday	Thursday
Clothes Laid Out					
Lunch Packed					
Water Bottle Ready					
Homework Finished					
Backpack Packed					

In the Morning Before School:

	Monday	Tuesday	Wednesday	Thursday	Friday
Dressed					
Teeth Brushed					
Hair Combed					
Breakfast Eaten					
Bed Made					

At School:

	Monday	Tuesday	Wednesday	Thursday	Friday
Turn in Homework					
Prepare Materials (pencils, books, paper)					
Collect Homework and Books					
Bring Home Gym Clothes					
Bring Home Water Bottle and Lunch Bag					

"Take a look, Albert. I've made a list to help you keep track of all of the different things that you do throughout the day," his mother said.

"I think I understand," said Albert, feeling a little excited himself. "But why are there so many days?"

"It'll help you keep track of everything for the whole week," his mother explained. "For example, on Sunday night, after you lay your clothes out for school the next day, you can put a check mark in that

column. Do you understand?"

"Yeah, I think I do," said Albert with a smile. "This might just work!"

"Of course it will!" she reassured him. "Just take this notebook with you wher-ever you go. Don't forget to update it af-ter you do something, and then check to see what you still have to finish."

NOTE BOOK

The following Sunday evening, Albert was actually excited to start the new week. He knew that it was going to be better. He knew that he was going to be better.

And he was!

He didn't have one missing assignment.

He wasn't late for the bus, not even one morning.

He remembered his lunch and his water bottle every day.

By the end of the week, Albert was feeling pretty proud of himself. His mother was proud of him too.

That Sunday evening, Albert took out his notebook as he and his mother prepared for the coming week.

"Let's make some new charts for the week, shall we?" Albert's mother inquired.

"I already did it, Mom. We're all set!" Albert replied cheerily.

"Great, Albert! Let me take a look," she said.

Albert handed the notebook over to his mother, a little smile play-ing at the corners of his mouth.

Albert's mother thumbed through the notebook until she got to the lists. She wrinkled her brow, slightly confused as she looked over the notebook.

"What's this, Albert? A new chart?" she asked.

"Yep," said Albert, "take a closer look."

Now it was his mother's turn to smile. Albert had, indeed, added a new chart:

	Monday	Tuesday	Wednesday	Thursday	Friday
Thank Mom					

Plan your day ahead

Henry Calms Down

Henry had had a bad day. It started at breakfast time when he had spilled his father's coffee all over the table. He had been reaching for the butter when his elbow had hit the handle on his dad's coffee mug. It had toppled over on its side and a pool of brown liquid had begun to spread all over the table and drip onto the floor beneath the table.

"Henry, you've got to be more careful," urged his father as he used a napkin to dab at the dark stain spreading across the newspaper that had been lying on the table.

"Sorry, Dad," mumbled Henry.

"It's okay, son," reassured his father in a slightly annoyed voice, "just help me to clean up the table."

As he soaked up the brown, soggy mess, Henry felt a tightness begin in his body. It started in his chest and spread all the way through his shoulders, down his back, and into his arms. His breathing also became shallow and quicker than usual. He always experienced this uneven breathing and uncomfortable tightness in his muscles whenever he felt anxious or stressed out. Henry did not like how it felt.

Though Henry didn't like how his body responded when he felt anxious or nervous, he knew that it was pretty normal. His health teacher at school, Ms. Potter, had told his class how tight muscles, heavy breathing, and maybe even a stomach ache were all natural reactions to stress.

He finished his toast in silence and then made his way out of the door to swim practice, still feeling the uncomfortable feelings in his body.

By the time that Henry arrived at the swimming pool, he was beginning to feel a little better. It had been an accident, after all. His muscles had loosened a bit and he was ready to hit the water with the rest of his team.

Henry dove into the refreshing water. The cool water hit his body and he soon forgot about the coffee incident at breakfast.

Henry swam the entire length of the pool five times. His muscles had almost completely relaxed, and his breathing had steadied by the time that he stopped to rest.

He had noticed that any time that he was feeling nervous or anxious, running or swimming or kicking the soccer ball around always made him feel better.

After a good long practice, Henry was feeling completely back to himself. He got out of the pool and dried off, and then went to the locker room and changed back into his joggers and his t-shirt. He tied up his tennis shoes and slipped on his watch before gathering up his towel and heading back home.

Because Henry was feeling so much better, he decided to take the long way home through the park. He climbed the steep park steps to the park garden at the top of the hill. The garden always made Henry feel better too.

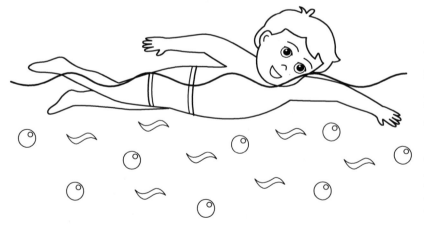

He sat down on a nearby park bench and enjoyed watching the morning sun shining through the garden. After admiring the view for several minutes, Henry glanced down at his watch. He'd better hurry if he wanted to make it home in time to catch the start of the baseball game on TV. His favorite team, the Seaside Dolphins, were playing for the championship title.

Henry skipped down the steps and headed toward home. He was a little surprised not to see his dog, Ginger, when he turned down his street. She was always waiting for him to return home.

The closer he got to the house, the more worried he became. He couldn't remember the last time that Ginger hadn't been there to meet him halfway down the block.

He walked a little faster, anxious to get home. His mother was watering her plants on the porch when Henry approached.

"Mom, have you seen Ginger today?" Henry asked, slightly panicked.

His mother looked up from her watering.

"Hmmm. Come to think of it, I haven't," she replied.

"I wonder where she is?" Henry asked, now more than slightly panicked. The tightness was starting. The muscles in his chest contracted. His shoulders and arms felt tense. His breathing became fast.

"Calm down, Henry. I'll help. We'll find her," his mother said.

"Let's go!" Henry exclaimed, heading back down the block.

They hadn't gone too far when, who should come bounding around the corner but Ginger!

"There you are!" shouted Henry as he ran toward the dog. "I was so worried!"

Ginger covered Henry's face in kisses, which made Henry feel better, but his shoulders were still tense, and his breathing didn't seem quite right.

Henry remembered how swimming had helped him to feel better when he had been anxious earlier that morning. Maybe a quick jog

would help too.

He clipped Ginger's leash to her collar and the two set off for a quick run around the block.

Almost as soon as Henry's feet began pounding the sidewalk, his breathing evened out. The more he ran, the more he loosened up.

He and Ginger ran around the block four times. By the time they arrived back home, Henry was tired, but he felt much better. He was breathing easier and his chest, back, shoulders, and arms felt relaxed.

It had taken more time than he'd thought to find Ginger and then calm his body down. Henry was hoping he'd still be able to catch the baseball game on TV. He glanced down at his watch to check the time.

He was unpleasantly surprised to find that his wrist was bare.

"Oh no!" thought Henry. "My watch! It's gone!"

Henry had saved for months to purchase the watch. It came equipped with a timer, a calculator, a flashlight, and even a tiny microphone. He had only just purchased the watch two weeks earlier. He couldn't believe that he already lost it!

The familiar tightness crept back through every muscle in Henry's body. It became difficult for him to breathe.

Henry was beginning to become very frustrated with all the challenges he'd faced that day, not to mention the uncomfortable manner in which his body was responding.

He didn't have time to think about that, though. He had to figure out where he had lost his watch.

Henry tried to slow his breathing and focus. He remembered that he had put it back on after swim practice. He also remembered glancing down at the time when he was in the garden at the park. He would start there!

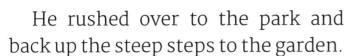

He rushed over to the park and back up the steep steps to the garden.

As soon as he cleared the top of the hill, Henry saw something silver glinting in the sun right next to the park bench on which he'd been sitting.

His watch! He ran over to the bench and bent down to pick it up.

He quickly secured the watch around his wrist as relief washed over him.

Though he was relieved, his body still felt uncomfortable. His muscles were still tight, and his breathing was still heavy. Just then, Henry spotted the steep steps.

Swimming had helped him to calm down after spilling his father's coffee.

Jogging had helped him to calm down after he'd thought Ginger was missing.

Henry was beginning to realize that exercise was good for his body when he was feeling tense or upset.

Maybe if he ran up and down those steps a few times he'd feel better.

Henry bounded down the steps, keeping his knees high and paying close attention to his breathing. When he got to the bottom of the stairs, he turned around and ran right back up. By the time he reached the bottom of the stairs for the third time, Henry was completely calm and relaxed. Exercising had worked again.

Henry glanced down at his watch one more time. If he hurried, he

may be able to catch the last half of the game on TV. Though hurrying was the last thing he wanted to do. Henry was tired from all that he had been through that day.

Instead, Henry walked slowly and calmly. His breathing was even and deep, and he felt more relaxed than he'd felt all day.

And he made it home just in time to see The Dolphins' big win!

Maybe his day wasn't so bad after all.

Take a deep breath and calm down

Don't Give Up

Wesley looked up to a lot of people in his life.

He thought that his art teacher, Mr. O'Toole, was patient and very creative.

He thought that his math teacher, Mr. Linley, was super-smart and great at explaining hard things.

He thought that the school principal, Mr. Barros, was fair and responsible.

Of course, Wesley looked up to his father because he was just about the coolest dad around.

But more than anyone, Wesley looked up to his older brother Drew.

Drew was sixteen years old. He could drive. He could play the guitar. And he made the best grilled cheese sandwiches.

Wesley thought all of those things were pretty amazing. But more than all of that, Wesley loved to watch Drew when he played sports.

Drew was the quarterback on the football team.

Drew was the goalie on the soccer team.

Drew was the fastest runner on the track team.

It seemed like Drew was always the

quickest, strongest, and most talented player of every team that he was on.

Wesley wanted to be just like Drew.

Not only was Drew a fantastic athlete, but he was also very wise. He always gave Wesley the best advice.

Every time that Wesley tried something new, Drew always told him the same thing, "Just try your best and don't give up."

That sounded easy enough to Wesley.

He was excited to put Drew's advice to the test as Wesley's first football season drew near.

On the first day of football practice, Wesley was tackled four times.

He didn't give up.

At the next practice, he fumbled the ball, dropping it right on the fifty-yard line.

He still didn't give up.

At the next practice, he was able to hang onto the ball, but he got all mixed up and ran the ball toward the wrong end zone.

He still didn't give up.

Every practice for the entire football season was the same. He wasn't quite as fast as the other players, and he always seemed to be two plays behind. But Drew's advice always echoed through Wesley's mind, "Don't give up. Don't give up."

And he didn't.

Soon after the football season ended, Wesley was excited to start track, just like his brother.

When Drew found out that Wesley would be running on the track team, Drew reminded him "Just try your best and don't give up."

Wesley thought back to his experience with football. Surely, track would be easier for him.

On the first day of track practice, Wesley lost his footing and fell, face first, on the track.

He didn't give up.

At the next practice, he became winded before even making it around the track once. His side was burning, and he could barely breathe.

He still didn't give up.

At the next practice, he finally made it around the track, but he finished behind every other kid.

He still didn't give up.

Just like with the football practice, Wesley struggled for the entire track season. He never won a single race and left every practice feeling sore and exhausted. But Drew's advice still constantly rang in Wesley's ears, "Don't give up. Don't give up."

And he didn't.

As the track season was wrapping up and the soccer season was starting, Wesley was sure that he'd have more success with this sport.

When Wesley signed up for the soccer team, Drew, once more, told Wesley, "Just try your best and don't give up."

Wesley was beginning to understand that this was a lot harder than he had first thought.

On the first day of soccer practice, Wesley attempted to kick the ball and missed, falling right down on his bottom.

He didn't give up.

At the next practice, Wesley played goalie, just like Drew, but was unable to stop even one ball from going into the net.

He still didn't give up.

At the next practice, Wesley's foot finally made contact with the ball, but he couldn't get it past the opposing team's goalie.

He still didn't give up.

Soccer never got any easier for Wesley. His feet never seemed to move in the right direction, and his kicks were often out of control. Still, he heard his brother's advice in his mind, "Don't give up. Don't give up."

And he didn't.

By the time that the soccer season had finally ended, Wesley was feeling pretty down. All three sports that Wesley had tried that year had been really tough. Maybe he wasn't cut out to be an athlete like his brother.

One afternoon, Wesley sat quietly on the swing in the backyard, his head hanging low.

He looked up when he heard the back door open, and then shut again.

It was Drew.

Noticing the defeat on his brother's face. Drew sat down on the swing next to him.

"What's wrong, little brother?" asked Drew with concern in his voice.

"Nothing," said Wesley quietly.

"Come on," continued

Drew, "you can tell me. Maybe I can help."

"It's just that, you're so good at sports and I'm so bad. I just wanted to be like you, and instead, I messed up all the time," Wesley explained reluctantly.

"Hey, hey, hey, that's enough of that talk," countered Drew. "You're not bad at anything. In fact, I'm really proud of you."

"How could you be proud of me?" Wesley asked incredulously. "I was horrible at everything I tried."

"No, you weren't. You're just learning. I had a tough time the first few seasons I played sports too," explained Drew.

"You did?" Wesley questioned with surprise.

"Absolutely," said Drew. "But I never gave up. And neither did you. That is something to be proud of."

"I guess," replied Wesley, not feeling convinced.

"Think about this, Wesley," began Drew. "When you started football, you couldn't even hang on to the ball. By the end of the season, you'd made it down the entire field, even if you did go in the wrong direction. I'd say that's a major improvement."

"True," replied Wesley.

"And track!" continued Drew. "When the season started you got winded before making it around the track even once. By the end of the season, you made it all the way around. Who cares if you didn't get first place?"

"Yeah?" Wesley questioned, feeling a little better.

"Don't forget about soccer! You improved so much over the season! At the beginning, you couldn't even kick the ball. During that last game, I saw some pretty powerful kicks from you. You'll get past the goalie next year. I guarantee it," reassured Drew.

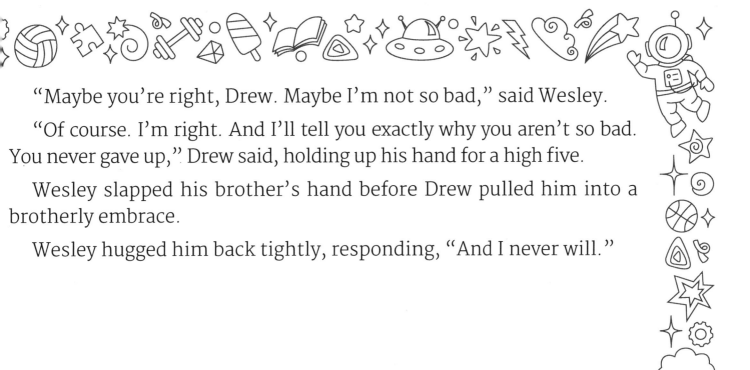

"Maybe you're right, Drew. Maybe I'm not so bad," said Wesley.

"Of course. I'm right. And I'll tell you exactly why you aren't so bad. You never gave up," Drew said, holding up his hand for a high five.

Wesley slapped his brother's hand before Drew pulled him into a brotherly embrace.

Wesley hugged him back tightly, responding, "And I never will."

Never give up

Jeremy's Jobs

Jeremy had lots of big jobs to do.

Ever since he had turned twelve, it seemed that things in life had gotten just a bit more challenging.

He had more responsibility at home.

There was more work to be done at school.

Even his piano lessons were more complicated than ever before.

Sometimes Jeremy felt a little overwhelmed with all of the things that he needed to do. When he felt overwhelmed, it was easy for him to just shut down completely and do nothing at all.

But that only made the problem worse. If he did nothing then the jobs just piled up, leaving Jeremy feeling even more overwhelmed.

It had become a real problem for Jeremy.

One afternoon, after a long day at school, Jeremy trudged home feeling very worn out. He thought that if he could just take a little nap before supper time then he might feel better.

When he opened his bedroom door, he was met with a huge mess. There were dirty clothes all over the floor and clean clothes stacked high on his dresser. His bed was unmade and there were several cups and dishes scattered around his bedside table. His mother had been telling him all week to clean up his room, but when he looked around, he just felt overwhelmed.

He stood motionless in the doorway, not even sure where to begin.

After several seconds, he felt a soft hand on his arm.

"Hi there," Jeremy's mom greeted him warmly. "Are you doing okay?"

"Look at my room. It's such a mess! I know that I should clean it, but I don't even know where to begin," Jeremy said, feeling defeated.

"It is kind of a mess, and I have been asking you to clean it all week. But we can figure this out together," she offered gently.

"How?" asked Jeremy.

"Let me tell you a secret. When I have a big job to do and I don't know where to begin, I break it down into lots of smaller jobs," she whispered playfully.

"I'm not sure that I understand," Jeremy said.

"Look around your room and tell me one thing that needs to be done," his mother instructed.

"But there are tons of things that need to be done," Jeremy replied.

"Let's just start with one thing, and then we'll go from there," she said.

Jeremy looked around the room.

"Well, there are lots of dirty dishes that need to go in the dishwasher," said Jeremy.

"Start there. Take all the dishes to the kitchen," she said.

Jeremy quickly gathered all of the dishes and took them into the kitchen. He was back in the bedroom in no time at all.

"Now we can move on to the next job," his mother explained.

"I think I understand. It does feel a lot less overwhelming to think of it as lots of tiny jobs instead of one huge job," said Jeremy as he placed his socks in the dresser drawer.

"That's right! And if you don't get everything done before supper,

that's okay. You have plenty of time," she said before disappearing down the hall to start on dinner.

To his surprise, he actually did finish before supper!

First, he cleaned up the dishes.

Then he put away his clean clothes.

Then he put his dirty clothes in the wash basket.

Finally, he made his bed.

Four little jobs were a lot easier than one big job.

After all of the dinner dishes had been washed, Jeremy sat down at the kitchen table and pulled out his homework.

Just looking at the huge stack of books and papers gave Jeremy an uncomfortable and familiar feeling. He had no idea where to begin, so he didn't begin. He just sat there, feeling overwhelmed.

As his mother was wiping up the last of the dinner crumbs from the kitchen table, she noticed Jeremy sitting as still as a statue in front of the pile of books.

"Feeling overwhelmed again?" she questioned.

"Yes!" responded Jeremy. "I have to read a chapter in my science book, finish all of the problems in my math notebook, and write three paragraphs about my favorite season for English class. There is no way that I can finish all of this."

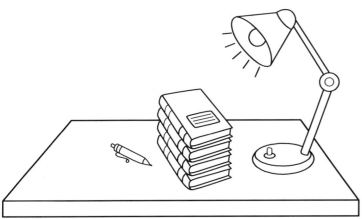

"Remember what I said earlier. Don't think of it as one big, impossible job. Think of it as three small, manageable jobs. Start with one and go from there," she reminded him.

"Do you think it will work for homework, too?" asked Jeremy.

"Of course it will. Now take your time and start small," she replied.

Jeremy thought about it for a moment. He actually liked to write, so it wouldn't be so bad to start with the season assignment from English class.

He quickly finished this and moved on to the math problems, which didn't take him nearly as long as he thought.

After completing all of the problems, he took a little ice cream break before moving on to his reading for science, which he finished in no time at all!

Three little jobs were a lot easier than one big job.

Jeremy went to bed that night feeling energized, and a lot less overwhelmed than he'd felt in days.

That is, until he woke up the next morning. It was Wednesday. He had piano lessons after school every Wednesday.

He knew that his instructor, Mrs. Lamont, would have a new piece for him to learn. He dreaded the lesson, and the new piece, all day.

When he pushed open the studio door at 4:00, he was already feeling overwhelmed, before she'd even introduced the new lesson.

"Hello, Jeremy, how are you today?" greeted Mrs. Lamont.

"Alright, I guess. Kind of stressed out about learning the new piece," Jeremy answered honestly.

"That's okay, Jeremy," replied Mrs. Lamont. "We all feel

overwhelmed sometimes."

As soon as Mrs. Lamont had said the word "overwhelmed", Jeremy remembered his mother's secret from the night before.

"That's it!" thought Jeremy, feeling relieved. "I just have to break down the one big job of learning the new piece into lots of little jobs!"

Instantly, Jeremy's attitude changed as he sat down at the piano. He started by just learning the first stanza of the music. He played it over and over until he felt comfortable.

After several minutes, he moved on to the next stanza, which was a little easier to learn now that he was familiar with the music.

Jeremy broke the entire piece down into lots of little pieces and, before the end of the lesson, he'd played the whole thing through—twice!

He couldn't wait to tell his mother how well her little secret had worked.

He ran all the way home from the music studio to find his mother sitting at the kitchen table buried in a stack of bills and junk mail.

"Mom! Guess what? I learned a new piece during my piano lesson today!" exclaimed Jeremy.

"That's great, Honey. It really is. Maybe you can play it for me later. I just don't have the time right now. I don't know how I'm ever going to make it through this mess," she replied, waving a defeated arm in the direction of the kitchen table, littered with piles of paper.

Jeremy had an idea.

"Let me tell you a little secret. Just start with one thing, one small thing, and then move on from there," he whispered.

Jeremy's mother looked up from the papers in front of her and smiled warmly at her son.

"Do you think it will work for me, too?" she asked playfully.

"Of course!" he replied.

"You're a really smart kid," she said as she smiled and tousled his hair.

"It's because I've got a really smart mom," Jeremy smiled back. "Now let's get busy!"

You are doing great with your tasks

Thank you for buying our book!

If you find this storybook fun and useful, we would be very grateful if you could post a short review on Amazon! Your support does make a difference and we read every review personally.

If you would like to leave a review, just head on over to this book's Amazon page and click "Write a customer review."

Thank you for your support!

Printed in Great Britain
by Amazon

14865926R00047